The Root of All Evil
By
Mark Stephen O'Neal

The Chronicles of Brock Lane
(based on the novella *Ulterior Motives*)

Copyright 2018 © Mark Stephen O'Neal

This is a work of fiction that contains imaginary names, characters, places, events, and incidents not intended to resemble any actual persons, alive or dead, places, events or incidents. Any resemblances to people, places, events, or incidents are entirely coincidental.

The Root of All Evil
All Rights Reserved

This book may not be reproduced, transmitted, or stored in whole or in part by any means, including graphic, electronic, or mechanical, without the express written consent of the author/publisher, Mark O'Neal Books, except in the case of brief quotations embodied in critical articles and reviews.

TABLE OF CONTENTS

Prologue

I sat down at the bar inside Chili's Grill and Bar in Calumet City, Illinois and ordered a beer and a shot of whiskey. It was unusually empty at first for a Friday night, and all the HD televisions had the Houston Rockets vs. the Phoenix Suns basketball game on. The Rockets disposed of my team, the St. Louis Trojans, in seven games, and I couldn't bear to watch them play because the wounds of defeat were still fresh in my mind. My routine was to go to Chili's when I arrived back in town from college or when I finished playing pro basketball by late spring. I haven't tasted an alcoholic beverage in five years, but today's drama gave me a good reason to drink.

"Would you like some hot wings or some other appetizer with your drinks?" the waitress asked.

"No, thanks," I said, still mulling over what took place moments ago.

"Are you okay?"

"No, I'm not. I just want my drinks, please."

"What happened, honey?" the waitress inquired. "Do you want to talk about it?"

She was a stunningly attractive young woman, who looked at me with eyes like a nurturing and concerned mother. She also looked familiar, but I couldn't place her face at first. A lack of appetite coupled with no sleep equaled a clouded brain.

"Look, I don't mean to be rude," I said, "but I need to get as drunk as humanly possible at this present moment. If you don't mind, I rather not talk about it. Thanks for asking, though."

"Very well," she said, looking very disappointed. "I'll bring your drinks right away. Sorry I bothered you."

She had a perplexed look on her face, like she knew me and was baffled because I didn't recognize her. Maybe she's from the old neighborhood, or maybe we went to the same church, I thought. But then it hit me—this five-foot ten beauty was Naomi Hill. I had a huge crush on her when we were in college, but I didn't act on my

1

feelings because we were both attached to other people at the time. How was I going to save face now? She had changed her hair color from black to auburn brown and had gained some weight, and the once slim model-like beauty was now a curvaceous size 12.

I looked and felt like a train wreck—the kind of feeling you get when you're completely burned out. But this felt a hundred times worse. I was also angry and confused about what just happened to me.

I suddenly reflected upon the street life I led when I was a teenager and how my biological father would beat me when I was a kid on a regular basis in an attempt to toughen me up. When I was eight, he showed me how to cook an *eightball* and taught me how to jam someone's nasal bone into his brain before he'd slap me around for not properly reciting the definitions of words he assigned for me to memorize. He had groomed me to be an educated thug—a carbon copy of himself, if you will.

"I want you to give me the definition of a coward," my father ordered. "If you get it right, I'll take you to get some ice cream. But if you answer incorrectly, I'm gonna beat you like a drum."

"Yes, sir," I said, trembling.

"Hurry up, dammit!"

"Coward...a person who lacks courage to do or endure dangerous or unpleasant things..."

"That's right, Son, very good. I'm not raisin' any punks. You hear me?"

"Yes, sir..."

"You can't be a coward in this world...these vultures will chew you up and spit you out for breakfast. Come on, let's get you an ice cream cone."

I snapped out of my trance before Naomi brought my drinks, and I gulped down the whiskey shot without hesitation. The whiskey burned as it went down my throat, and it burned even more as it entered my stomach. I haven't slept or eaten since Thursday morning, and I began to sweat profusely.

"Thank you," I said.

"Let me know if you need anything else, okay?" she asked. "Anything."

I nodded as I wiped my face with a napkin. I immediately followed my shot with the beer and finished it in a minute flat. I sat still momentarily before I flagged down Naomi for another round. She just finished taking orders from people who arrived a few minutes after I did, and the crowd was starting to pick up. I was also trying to think of a way to smooth things over with her.

"Hit me again," I requested.

"Okay," she said. "Do you just want a shot or a shot and beer?"

"Give me a double shot with the beer. Thank you."

"You're welcome. I'll bring your drinks right away."

Feeling inebriated would temporarily numb the pain I was feeling, but I knew I'd pay for it later. I also hoped no one would recognize me because I was in no mood for autograph signing. That wouldn't have been a problem two seasons ago, when I was at the end of the bench. I would have just blended in with a t-shirt, jeans, and Nike Air Jordan 1987 edition shoes. I figured that, as long as I stayed in my seat, nobody would notice me. However, that was going to be next to impossible because I felt a bathroom break coming on very soon as the beer and whiskey began to take a toll on my bladder. I also started feeling lightheaded because of the alcohol and sleep deprivation, and I was certainly not thinking clearly because rage had totally consumed my mind.

I was definitely at a crossroad. There I was, Brock Lane, a twenty-five-year-old NBA superstar, faced with the biggest decision I would ever make in this juncture of my short existence. Whatever happened next would change my life forever.

Chapter 1

Yesterday

I arrived at the Lambert International Airport an hour before my flight and was anxious to get back to Chicago to see my family. Even though we didn't advance out of the first round of the playoffs, everyone was expecting us to be the up-and-coming contenders for next season. I also had a breakout season at point guard—following up my twenty points and five assists per game last season with twenty-five points and six and a half assists per game this season after spending the first two years on the pine, and my phone was ringing off the hook from potential endorsement deals. Not bad for the last pick in the 2014 Draft from Union College.

I owned a condo in downtown St. Louis, and my complex consisted mostly of a melting pot of young, urban professionals. I considered myself to be a low-key type of person, who kept to himself most of the time. I didn't talk to anyone outside of greeting them for the first two years of living in St. Louis, but as my stock began to rise, I had no choice but to be a little friendlier when I was approached by neighbors. Alison James, who was my next-door neighbor, befriended me over a period of time while living at the complex. She would get my mail when I was away and prepared an occasional home-cooked meal for me when the team was in town. She was like a mother to me and would encourage me during the dog years of riding the bench, and I really appreciated her for it.

Everything I needed was within walking distance—there was a movie cinema, several grocery and convenient stores, fine dining, a mall, and the stadium was right in the middle of downtown St. Louis. I could also hop on the Interstate and be at the airport in about thirty minutes.

I had a little time to kill before my flight, so I walked toward one of the kiosks to buy bottled water and a newspaper. The airport was somewhat crowded for a Thursday because of Mother's Day weekend, and I got two autograph requests in a matter of fifteen minutes. I didn't mind because I had gotten used to being approached by adoring fans, and I was just enjoying being free of my hectic schedule for a few weeks.

"Brock Lane!" shouted an enthusiastic fan. "Can I please have your autograph? You are my favorite player on the Trojans."

"Sure, no problem. What's your name?"

"Joe...Joe Hawkins. Here, you can sign this notebook, please."

Joe,

Thank you for your generous support.

Brock Lane

"Thank you so much. I hope the Trojans win it all next year."

"Thanks, Joe, we'll surely give it our best shot."

I shook Joe's hand, and I walked toward my departure gate to wait on my flight. The city of St. Louis expected great things from the Trojans next season, and all I could think about was the pressure of bringing home the city's first championship. Minutes later, my cell phone rang, but I didn't know the number.

"Hello?"

"Hi, Brock, how are you?"

"Is this Autumn?" I said, surely with a very puzzled look on my face.

"Yeah, silly, you don't recognize my voice?" she said cheerfully.

"No, it's not that...it's just that it's been four years since we talked. You totally caught me by surprise."

Autumn Montgomery was my college sweetheart for almost three years, but her family never approved of me because of where I grew up—the south side of Chicago. Autumn comes from Virginia's Black aristocracy, so I clearly wasn't from the right pedigree, according to her family. Three weeks after our junior year, she broke up with me and started dating some investment banker. I decided to enter the NBA Draft after that and hadn't seen or spoken to her since.

"I see your cell number hasn't changed," she said. "I figured it was a shot in the dark that I'd catch you."

"Why would it?" I said calmly. "I'm not hiding from anyone."

"Can we meet somewhere and talk? There's a lot I want to say...I want to apologize for everything."

"There's nothing to say, really. Besides, I'm flying to Chicago today, and I won't be back for at least a month."

"Hey, baby, I'm truly sorry, and I didn't mean to leave you hanging like I did. It's just that...I was young and immature, and I wasn't woman enough to stand up to my family regarding you."

"It's fine, Autumn, because I'm over it. I have to admit that you had me messed up for a minute, though."

"I want you to know that Andre and I are over because I could never love him the way I love you. I want us to be a couple again."

"I'm afraid that's not possible. You can't just call me out of the blue and expect me to drop everything that I got going on..."

"Are you seeing someone right now?"

"That's really none of your business," I said, my voice raising an octave.

"Why can't we just pick up where we left off?" she asked aggressively. "Look, I said I was sorry..."

"You do realize that we weren't in a good place, right? Why on earth would I want to go back to that?"

"I don't want to leave things like this, Brock. I realize I still love you."

"It's not always about what you want. It took me a long time to forgive you, but I had to in order to stay sane and move on. I beat myself up for months, wondering what I did wrong. But then it hit me...it's just like basketball. You can hold your head up high with no regrets when you give everything you have, win or lose."

"So, you forgive me?"

"Yes, Autumn, I forgive you, but I can never forget about what happened between us."

"Well, since you've forgiven me, let's make up for lost time..."

"I'm not breaking my rules for you or anybody else. I'm not going to be intimate with anyone again until marriage."

"What are you saying? You're telling me that you found God?"

"Yes, I have."

"I don't buy it...you're just saying that because you don't want me anymore."

"This isn't a joke, Autumn. We can't pick up where we left off ever again."

"What if I don't want to be just friends?"

"That's fine with me because I really don't care what you want."

"I'm just kidding, Brock, relax. Friends it is."

"Okay, you take care of yourself," I said, rushing to get off the phone.

"I will," she said coyly. "Bye."

A part of me was glad Autumn called because it allowed me to release any residual feelings of anger I had toward her. Now, I can truly move on without looking back. However, I'm not blind to the fact that she probably called because of my new contract extension.

A few moments later, my cell phone rang again. I checked my caller ID and saw it was my stepfather.

"Hey, Dad."

"Hey, Brock, what time does your flight get here?"

"My flight lands at ten thirty," I said after I yawned. "I'm going to take a quick nap as soon as I get on the plane. I've been up since six."

"Well, you come home and relax as long as you want. I'm so proud of you, Son."

"Thanks, Dad. I'll see you in an hour or so."

"Okay."

My stepfather's name is Brent Jones, and he's been in my life since I was twelve. He married my mother Joyce shortly afterward, but she died of breast cancer three years later...God rest her soul. My younger sister's name is Jasmine Lane—and she just finished undergrad with a degree in accounting at USC. We're three years apart.

My stepfather has been a solid rock in our lives, since my mother died ten years ago. Nicole, who is the oldest of my stepfather's children, made partner at the most prestigious law firm in the Washington D.C. area. Nicole and I showed him our gratitude by pitching in and buying him a new home in Manteno, Illinois and a brand-new BMW.

My stepfather also has a son—Brent Jr. Junior is a twenty-three-year-old convicted felon, who's always in trouble, and he's out of jail to serve the remainder of his five-year bid on house arrest for drugs and weapons charges.

Suddenly, I found it extremely difficult to keep my eyes open. My motor had been running nonstop since training camp last October, and I was in desperate need of a break.

We are now boarding Flight 124 for Chicago. Please have your boarding pass ready...

I got up from my seat to board the plane when I saw my teammate Malik Thomas about to get in line ahead of me. He was the superstar power forward of the Trojans, who was second on the team in scoring, and he led the team in rebounding. He was drafted a year ahead of me and was already enjoying the fruits of his lucrative contract extension.

"Malik!" I shouted.

"Hey, what's up, Brock?" he asked. "What are you doing here?"

"I'm on my way to Chicago to see my dad and little brother. What do you have going on this weekend?"

"I met this gorgeous chick, named Tanya Ross, downtown at lunchtime a couple of days ago. She was in town for the breast cancer awareness conference at the Marriot Hotel. She's from Chicago, and she invited me to visit her."

"Wow, that's great, man. How long are you going to be in town?"

"Just for the weekend. Hey, you've got to come to this party with me on Saturday. It's at a secret location on the northside, and Paul Carter and Brian Dawson of the Chicago Bulls are throwing it. Are you down?"

"Yeah, I'm down. What time are you going to the party?"

"Probably around ten or eleven. Where does your dad stay?"

"In Manteno."

"Damn, what a coincidence. Tanya stays in Park Forest. That's not too far from you. I can scoop you up at nine thirty, and we can head over there."

"Hey, man, how the hell does a native New Yorker like you know your way around Chicago so well?"

"What can I say? I get around."

We both laughed at his remark. As we approached the entrance to the plane, the ticket agent was staring at us with a big smile on her face. Suddenly, some of the passengers, in addition to the ticket agent, started clapping and cheering for us.

"Congratulations on a terrific season, gentlemen," the ticket agent said. "Can I have both of your autographs?"

"Of course, you can," I said.

"Me, too," a passenger said.

"Sure, no problem," Malik said.

As we were signing autographs, I couldn't help but think about how blessed we were to have the life we were living. I was in a great place now after all the hardships and pain I've experienced throughout my life. After we finished signing about a dozen autographs, we boarded the plane and claimed our seats in first class. Coincidently, Malik had a window seat on the right side of the plane directly across from my window seat. I had got a burst of energy after signing autographs—forgetting how tired I was moments ago.

"When did you start flying first class, man?" Malik asked.

"Now that I'm about to get this *phat* contract extension, I don't have to pinch pennies anymore," I replied.

"Good for you. Now that you aren't afraid to hang out with the big spenders, you can accompany me to the boat tonight."

"I thought you were visiting Tanya this weekend. Sounds like you're going to be in the streets the whole time."

"Don't get it twisted, man. Going to the boat is my routine whenever I come to Chicago. A couple of hours at the Hammond casino, and I'm out. After that, Tanya has my undivided attention for the rest of the weekend."

"So, you're bringing sand to the beach on Saturday, huh?"

"Yeah, man...a true playa can mack with or without a girl on his arm. You can bring someone and make it a double."

"I'm not seeing anyone right now...I guess I'm gonna fly solo."

"No worries. I'm sure Tanya has some friends you could hook up with."

"I guess I could do the blind-date thing," I said reluctantly.

"Relax, dude, it'll be fine."

"I'm cool."

Malik paused and said, "Speaking of hookups, when are you going to hook me up with one of your gorgeous sisters, homeboy?"

"Never," I answered. "I'm not letting you anywhere near Nikki or Jaz, playa," I said, laughing as I watched the ramp personnel load the luggage.

"Ah, come on, man...my intentions are strictly honorable. When I saw Jaz for the first time, it was love at first sight for me, bro. Now that she's finished with school, maybe she'll have time to give a brother like me a shot."

"You're kidding, right?" I asked as my body temperature had quickly risen to a dangerous level.

"Calm down, bro," he carefully replied. He could clearly sense I wasn't joking.

"You need to focus on getting to know Tanya, *amigo*."

"You're right, my brother. No disrespect."

"It's cool."

I didn't say anything else the remainder of the flight and fell asleep before the flight attendant could give her pre-flight safety drill. I loved Malik like a brother, but he always seemed to make stupid remarks more often than not.

We arrived at the Peotone Airport in about forty-five minutes, and we walked over to baggage claim together. The Peotone Airport is about the size of Midway Airport, and we retrieved our luggage in no time.

"I'll call you on Saturday when I'm on my way to get you," he said.

"Cool, I've got some running around to do in the afternoon, but I'll be home around six."

"Alright. Hey, do you need a ride to your dad's house?"
"No, thanks. My dad is coming to get me."
"Okay, I'll see you Saturday."
"Peace, my brother."

Chapter 2

I reached for my phone to let my stepfather know I arrived at the airport. Malik and I had gotten our luggage from baggage claim about five minutes earlier, and he took off.

"My flight just arrived about fifteen minutes ago," I said, wiping some sweat from my brow.

"I'm double-parked right in front of Terminal One," Brent said.

"Okay, I'm coming right out."

I grabbed my luggage and started walking toward the exit. The balmy weather felt great—seventy degrees, sunny and not too humid. It was ninety degrees in St. Louis, and it wasn't even June yet.

"Hello, Son," Brent said.

"How have you been, Dad?" I asked, giving him a hug.

"I've been good. How was your flight?"

"It was short...I felt asleep on the plane about fifteen minutes in."

"Good. Make sure you get as much rest as you need for the next few weeks."

"That's the plan."

There was momentary silence, and Brent said, "I saw some young lady pick up Malik outside. Was he on your flight?"

"Yeah, and I didn't even know he was coming to Chicago."

"How is he doing? He took the loss pretty hard at the press conference."

"Malik is alright. He's all business on the court, but he's a totally different person off the court."

"Come on, let's go. I don't want the cops giving me a ticket for being parked out here."

"You've got the ride shining, Dad...with all the bells and whistles. Did you just come from the carwash?"

"As a matter of fact, I did. There's no rain in the forecast all weekend, so I took a chance."

"It always seems to rain the day after I wash my car," I said.

"Ain't that the truth," he said. "Hey, do you want to go to Chili's and get some lunch?"

"Yeah, that's fine. I'm not quite a household name yet, so having some peace and quiet while dining out on a weekday isn't a remote possibility."

"You should just embrace your stardom, Son."

"I know, and I have. The life I used to know is gone forever."

Traffic was light on Interstate Fifty-Seven, and Chili's Grill and Bar was located in Calumet City—a forty-five-minute ride from the airport.

"Are you ever going to coach high school basketball again?" I asked. "I think you're great with kids because you taught me a lot."

"I don't know," he replied, "maybe. I'm really enjoying retirement right now."

"I understand. It's time to pass the torch to the next crop of coaches."

"I know you would make a great coach someday."

We both smiled. My stepfather had finally found the elixir to heal his broken heart. He was finally at peace with himself and adjusting to an empty nest before Junior came back home. He was at a point in his life where he could cherish all the memories of my mother without grieving. It took him a long time to get over her death.

Our smiles soon turned to immediate concern as we noticed a car had been following us since we left the airport. Nothing really stood out about the car—a rust-colored 1987 Caprice with tinted windows. But I did notice it had license plates that read *MR GRIM*.

"Did you notice that a car has been following us since we left the airport?" I asked.

"Yes, I noticed it by the time we merged on Interstate 80," Brent said. "We're three blocks away from the restaurant. I doubt anything will happen out here on Torrence Avenue."

"It doesn't matter where we are in Chicago—they jack cars in any part of the city and in any suburb—broad daylight or night. If they want the car, we have to give it up."

"You're absolutely right. It's a new day."

We parked in the lot in the rear of the restaurant, and the Caprice entered the lot and stopped right in front of my stepfather's car. We stood frozen as the passenger side window lowered and the barrel of a nickel-plated, nine-millimeter Glock was pointed directly at us. I could also smell the stench of marijuana coming from the car so strong that I was buzzed on contact and suddenly feared taking my next drug test.

"Get in the car," the passenger said.

"What's this about?" I asked. "If you want the car, take it."

"We don't want the car, Brock. I won't ask you to get in again."

My stepfather and I grudgingly sat down in the back seats—still high from the second-hand weed smoke.

"Do you know what you're doing?" I asked.

"I know exactly what I'm doing, my man," the passenger said. "Pay attention because I'm only going to say this once."

"Don't say another word, Brock," Brent said. "Let him talk."

"We are hit men contracted to collect one million dollars from you by tomorrow. And let me give you this warning...don't even think about going to the police because it's a cop who hired us for the job. We will take Mr. Jones as collateral, and if you fail to comply with our terms, he's as good as dead. We will meet you on a baseball diamond in the warehouse district off 126th and Torrence tomorrow at midnight. Now grab your father's phone and get out!"

I honored my stepfather's wishes by keeping my mouth shut as I climbed out of the back seat. I felt awkward as they sped off—I never allowed anyone, even after I got out of the drug game, to disrespect me like that until today. I had to eat my words because risking my stepfather's life wasn't an option.

I felt my blood boiling underneath the surface of my skin as I began to think of ways of killing them both. The past I kept buried for seven years had resurfaced in a way unimaginable—the kidnapping of my stepfather. It was a very bold move to abduct us in the Chili's parking lot, and unfortunately, they were smart enough to know that a cell phone was traceable.

I stood in the parking lot for at least five minutes—totally forgetting the fact that I was a born-again Christian. Why was a dirty cop trying to bleed money out of me? Maybe it's someone from the task force sent to take down my crew seven years ago. Someone knew my flight information and where to find me. The clock was ticking, and I had to come up with a game plan. I had to know who was behind this, and I knew I needed a wolf to catch a wolf without involving the police.

Chapter 3

Naomi had to work the nine to three o'clock shift at a mom-and-pop's breakfast diner in Calumet City. It was six hours at the diner, and then it was off to an accounting class at Roosevelt University from six to nine. Her weekly schedule was filled to capacity with work and school, and she was six hours from graduation, once she took her final exam at the beginning of next week.

"I'm going to need you to work tomorrow, Naomi," her boss said. "Cindy called in sick today, and she's in the hospital."

"Come on, Steve, you know I have class all day tomorrow," she said. "I'm swamped as it is."

"I really need you to come in tomorrow, Naomi...I have no one else I can count on. I'll pay you double for the day if you do this favor for me."

"Let me have Saturday off, so I can study for my finals, and you have a deal."

"Okay, you got it. I really appreciate this."

"Do you mind if I take my lunch now? I have some important errands to run."

"Sure, go ahead."

Naomi left to take her car to the shop for new brakes, and she had to pay her electric bill. Her plan was to pay her bill first, drop her car off at the shop, and take an Uber back to the diner. She hoped her car would be ready by the time she finished her shift at three, but she already had a plan B, which was to take an Uber downtown to class.

Her cell phone rang as she was parking her car at the Firestone in Lansing, Illinois. She checked her caller ID and saw it was her friend and sorority sister, Cecilia.

"What's up, girl?" Naomi asked.

"Nothing much," Cecilia answered, "just checking up on you. I haven't heard from you in a while."

"I'm alright...just juggling school and work; that's all."

16

I was calling to let you know I'll be in town tomorrow to visit my folks. What do you have going on?"

"I would have had class tomorrow until three, but I have to work until three instead. My weekend officially starts after that. I also have to study for finals, but I'll still be able to hang out with you."

"Okay, maybe we can go shopping or catch a movie."

"That sounds good."

Cecilia paused for a moment and asked, "So, what's up with your love life, girl?"

"What love life? I don't really have time for that."

"Damn, Nae Nae, you're just gonna let life pass you by. There are too many fine brothers in Chicago...definitely more to choose from there than in Grand Rapids, Michigan."

"At least you have a great job working in your field, CeCe. Having a man isn't everything."

"I get it...you're still pining over Brock..."

"Girl, you're crazy...I'm not even thinking about him anymore. No sense fantasizing about something that's never gonna happen."

"Who do you think you're fooling? You compare every single guy you meet to him, and you two have never even gone out on a date. You really need to let that go."

"I already have. I have to go, CeCe, so call me when you arrive at the airport on Friday. I can pick you up if you don't have a ride."

"Thanks, girl, I will. Talk to you later."

"Bye."

Chapter 4

The contract killers drove Brent Sr. to a secret location somewhere in Indiana. They turned out to be somewhat hospitable in spite of the circumstances because they stopped at the McDonald's on 162nd and Cottage Grove and bought Brent a Quarter Pounder combo meal. They blindfolded and handcuffed him after they finished eating.

"I hope you're comfortable back there, Brent," the driver said.

"I'm fine, despite being bound and blindfolded," Brent said. "Let me ask you something...how do you guys make a profit by smoking the stuff you're supposed to be selling?"

"That's a good question, Brent," the passenger riding shotgun answered. "What makes you think we sell drugs?"

"Come on, man, it's always drugs. Too many Black men feel like slinging dope is the only way to make a living in this country."

"For your information, pops, we don't sell drugs," the driver said. "We're paid strictly to kill people."

"That's even worse," Brent said with a look of disgust.

"What gives you the right to be so damn self-righteous?" the passenger asked. "No one said a thing while we were killing Iraqis over in Baghdad. We merely take the scraps this country gives us."

"You served in the Gulf?" Brent asked.

"Yeah, Brent, and there wasn't a band or a job waiting for us back home after serving two tours of duty," the passenger answered.

"That's an honorable thing," Brent said. "I'm an ex-marine, too...I served in the Gulf War in 1991."

"I thought you looked kind of young to be Brock's father," the driver said. "How old are you, about forty-five?"

"Fifty," Brent answered.

"Yeah, you look more like Brock's older brother than his father," the passenger added.

"While we're getting acquainted, you know, being all friendly and hospitable," the driver said, "if I have to kill you because Brock can't deliver the goods, I won't hesitate, even though I won't like it."

"That goes double for me," the passenger added.

"I'm touched, fellas. I really am," Brent said with slight indignation.

They pulled up in front of what appeared to be a shack in one of the roughest neighborhoods in Gary, Indiana. There were a few apartments, some vacant lots, a couple of abandoned buildings, and a grocery store on the corner. There was broken glass and trash everywhere—a street-cleaning truck hadn't been down the block in months. This was going to be Brent's home for the next couple of days. It was a little past noon, and all was quiet—for now.

Chapter 5

I decided to comb my old neighborhood to find out some answers. I hoped someone from my past could help me with the one clue I had—an Illinois license plate that read *MR GRIM*. Jesse Owens Park was a good place to start, and it was located on Eighty-Seventh and Jeffery Boulevard with the neighborhood high school across the street. I honed my skills on those basketball courts, and watching the next crop of young stars brought back some great memories.

I parked on the south side of Eighty-Seventh Street and got out to watch some of the guys play. I didn't recognize any of them because I hadn't stepped foot in this park in a few years. That was when I noticed Blue, a guy who went to the same grammar school I did, watching the game on the other side of the basketball court. He was a year ahead of me, but he looked much older—like life had dealt him a bad hand. He had forty ounces of liquid crack in his left hand and a Newport in his right.

He had been in and out of jail over the years, with a rap sheet as long as my arm, and I had some street credibility with him because of my two-year stint in the drug game. Once I saw him, I decided to walk toward him to see if he would recognize me before I said anything to him. He looked in my direction with a big grin on his face, and by then, I knew that he figured out who I was.

"My man Brock," Blue said.

"How have you been, Blue?" I asked, giving him a firm handshake and a hug.

"I've been cool, man...trying to keep my head up, bro. Hey, good job this season, man. You had the Rockets on the ropes, and that was the best game seven I ever watched. That damn Flash Tucker was just unstoppable, though."

"Thanks, Blue. It wasn't easy guarding him. I was able to bother his shot somewhat, but he's so quick."

"Yeah, man, you checked him about as good as anybody could."

"Yeah, you're right. No one was going to stop him that night. It looks like we got some talent out here, huh?"

"A couple of all-state players, you know. That guy in the green Nike t-shirt is Derrick Palmer, and he's going downstate to Union next year. You may wanna talk to him and give him some advice or something."

"That's a good idea, Blue. I will. But before I do that, do you know anything about a guy who drives a Caprice with the license plate *MR GRIM?*"

"*MR GRIM,*" he said, pondering the name.

"Yeah, an old beat up, rust-colored Caprice," I said, hoping to jar his memory.

"Nope. Never heard of him. Hey, did they threaten you...because I can put the word out."

"No, nothing like that. I was just wondering...I met him at a party a couple of days ago, and they were asking questions about some of the guys from the old neighborhood; that's all."

"Oh, okay. Before you go, I just want to say I'm proud of you, man. Most of us didn't make it out of here, but you did."

"Thanks again, Blue. That means a lot to me."

I shook Blue's hand again and walked toward Derrick Palmer to introduce myself. He instantly recognized me, and he asked me to sign his jersey. I gave him the rundown on Union College—the pitfalls, pro and cons of the school. We talked for about fifteen minutes before I decided it was time to call Will to find out who these mystery men were and who their employer was.

I waited a second or two for my cell to get a good signal before I called him. I hadn't spoken to him in a couple of weeks because my schedule has been very busy.

"Will," I said.

"Is that you, Brock?" he asked. "How you been, man?"

"Yeah, Will, of course it's me. Who else would it be?"

"What's wrong, bro?"

"Can you meet me at Jesse Owens Park right now?"

"Sure, give me about ten minutes. What's going on?"

"I'll tell you about it when you get here."

"Alright, peace."

"Peace."

Wilbur Johnson was my best friend, and we have known each other since high school. He hates his first name, so everyone calls him Will for short. We were teammates on the high school basketball team all four years. Bull was the enforcer on the team who gave us the toughness needed to win two State Championships.

Once Will graduated from high school, his life took a different turn than mine. We both got probation for selling drugs, but he chose to remain in the streets, instead of going to college. Union College almost backed out of giving me a scholarship, but my stepfather's ties to the school, coupled with the fact that I was able to convince the administration I'd turned over a new leaf, turned the tide in my favor.

I continued to watch the guys play basketball until Will arrived at the park, and some Hispanic young men were playing soccer on the football field several yards away. It continued to be a beautiful day weather-wise—seventy-five degrees and little breezier than it was at the airport because I was close to Lake Michigan—about three miles north of the park or two miles in the eastern direction.

"Hey, Will!" I shouted, waving my arms in the air to get his attention.

"What's up, dawg?" Will shouted back with a big smile on his face, and we gave each other a firm handshake and a hug, the customary Black man's greeting. "It's so good to see you. Anyway, congratulations on a great season."

"Thanks, man."

"So, what's going on, Brock?"

"Two guys kidnapped my dad, and they want one million dollars by Friday at midnight or else he's dead."

"Kidnapped?"

"Yeah, and they're driving an '87 Caprice with *MR GRIM* on the license plates, and the passenger pointed this old-school, nickel-plated *Nina* at my dad and me. I was hoping you knew who they were."

"Give me some time to ask around."

"Time isn't on my side, bro. I'll kill them if I have to."

"Calm down, man...you're no killer. Besides, you have too much to lose, so let me handle this."

"I'm no choirboy, either."

"I know you ain't no saint, my brother, because our drug game was tight, remember?"

"We were smalltime hustlers, Will—selling just enough to get by. Besides, if we were moving any real weight, we'd still be locked up. Anyway, how soon can you find out who they are?"

"I don't know but give me a few hours to see what I can find out on these streets. Hey, have you told Junior about what happened?"

"No, I haven't been home yet."

"Let's meet up at Pepe's Tacos across the street in about three hours, and we can tell him together, alright?"

"Alright. Thanks, man. I appreciate this."

"You don't have to thank me, Brock. I owe you...I owe you for everything. Don't worry, we're going to get your dad back."

Chapter 6

It had been over three hours, and I still hadn't heard anything from Will. I kept mulling the morning over and over in my head, but I came up with nothing. I perused neighborhoods on the southeast side of Chicago and south suburbs, like Dolton, Riverdale, and Harvey, to ask several other acquaintances about the hit men. Nobody knew one iota of information—it's almost like they were ghosts.

It was a little after four o'clock, so going home at that moment would be a possible nightmare because of rush hour. I drove back to the Pepe's Tacos parking lot and waited for Will. My appetite was nonexistent, and worry from the morning's events was starting to make me antsy. Finally, he entered the parking lot after waiting an hour.

"What did you find out, Will?" I asked.

"I talked to a friend of mine who's deep in the streets, and he told me these guys are paid assassins," he answered.

"Paid assassins?"

"Yes, paid assassins, contract killers, hit men, or whatever you want to call them. They'll smoke just about anybody for ten grand."

"Why me? I can't for the life of me figure out how they knew I was coming to Chicago today. The only person who knew my flight information was my dad, Will."

"You're a public figure, Brock. It's next to impossible for you to fly below the radar completely."

"But how did these two grimy dudes get my info, bruh? And what are their names?"

"I don't know, man."

"Your boy doesn't know their names?"

"Nobody knows their names...the only thing known about them is the code name Grim, which is short for Grim Reaper. When somebody wants a person erased, they hire the Grim Reaper."

"So, the Grim Reaper is a duo?"

"Yeah, as far as I know."

"How does one get in contact with them?"

"You don't find them...they find you once the word is put out."

"Who do you contact to put the word out?"

"That's classified information, Brock. You're either in or you're out...and if you're not in the streets, then you're out."

Will paused for a moment and said, "So, what are we going to do in the meantime?"

"I know Friday is a day away, so I've got to figure out how to come up with the rest of the money. I'm doing well, but I can't even come close to putting my hands on that kind of cash today."

"How much do you have right now?"

"All I've got is about two hundred fifty grand in my operating account at Chase Bank, and fifty thousand in my safe back in St. Louis. The rest of my money is tied up in stocks, bonds, and mutual funds."

"That's it? But I thought you just signed that huge contract extension for $150 million..."

"Effective next season, remember?"

"Oh yeah, right...but I thought you were still a millionaire, though."

"Damn, Will, do I need to give you a numerical breakdown of my finances?"

"Please enlighten me, brother, because I was under the assumption that *all* NBA players were millionaires."

"Okay, man, let me educate you. I made the league minimum of eight hundred grand for three years before I signed my extension—which totaled about 2.4 million. Roughly half of that went to taxes, and I get taxed in every state I play in. Also, factor in that a good portion of the rest of my money is tied up in stocks, bonds, and mutual funds, and you of all people should know I spend a great deal of time, money, and energy helping out friends and family whenever I can."

"Yes, I do," Will said, scratching his head, "and I appreciate your investment in my barbershop, bro."

"Most people don't understand how things really work in the NBA. I was the last pick in my draft class, and many of the second-round players like me don't last long enough to get that next contract. If you can hang around past four years, you're good."

"I now have a newfound understanding of your situation, Brock."

"I appreciation your sentiment, but I need to come up with some ideas on how to raise this money."

"I wish I had some cash for you, but I only got $5,000 in the bank."

"Don't worry about it. The info you gave me is worth just as much as money. Thanks."

"No problem. Anything I can do to help, let me know."

"Okay."

"So, what's your next move?" Will asked, rubbing the beard on his   chin.

"Time is running out, so I'm gonna get my money out of the bank tomorrow," I answered. "That'll give me 250 grand to start, but I don't know how I'm gonna get the rest of the money."

"What about your cash in St. Louis?"

"It's not worth the time and effort to fly there and drive back with the cash, and besides, that fifty thousand will only put me at 300 grand."

"Have you told Junior about what's going on yet?"

"Nope, not yet."

"Come on, we can tell him together."

"No, man, you done enough already. I can handle it from here."

"Come on, Brock, let me help you...I have a plan."

"What's your plan?"

"I'll tell you about it when we get to your dad's house."

"Okay."

I began plotting how I was going to come up with the rest of the money. I was able to talk to my broker before the close of business, and there was no way to access my money before Monday.

I also began to think about how much easier life was when I was in college en route to my stepfather's house. Conversely, my life in my junior year of high school was in turmoil after my mom's death, and I turned to the streets as a way to cope with my loss. It was by the grace of God that I didn't do any time in prison. And my stint at Union College was the fresh start I needed to turn my life around. The best years of my life were the four years I spent in college because the only two things I had to worry about were studying and basketball.

Chapter 7

Brent was sitting on a bed with his arm handcuffed to an iron, grill-like headboard that was connected to two wooden bedposts. The hit man driver was sitting in a chair across the room watching *The Jerry Springer Show* on a thirty-seven-inch, HD television. The hit man passenger had stepped out for a moment—probably en route to score more marijuana, buy some takeout, or both.

"Let me know when you need a bathroom break," the hit man driver said.

"I'm alright for now," Brent answered. "What's with these handcuffs, man? I'm not going anywhere with that Rottweiler in the front living room."

"I'm not taking any chances, Brent. You are an ex-marine, and I don't know what tricks you have up your sleeve."

"Fair enough. Can we watch something besides this daytime drama? There has to be a game on or something."

"Jerry Springer is the joint, man. When it goes off, we can watch a baseball game or something, alright?"

"Alright. Let me ask you a question. Who has it out for my son?"

"That's classified information, Brent. My employer wishes to remain anonymous...strictly business, nothing personal."

"Don't be fooled by Brock's clean-cut image. He has a somewhat dirty past, and he *will* get to the bottom of this. You are underestimating him."

"I'm not the least bit worried about Brock. My employer knows everything there is to know, and that's that."

"Alright, whatever you say. If you don't mind me asking, how old are you?"

"I'm twenty-five."

"I see. You have an athletic build. Did you play football?"

"As a matter of fact, I did. I was an all-state running back and all-star shooting guard in California, and I tore my ACL at the end of my senior year in high school. All my scholarship offers dried up after that."

"I'm sorry to hear that, young man. I coached high school basketball for twenty years before I retired."

"So, did you play basketball when you were younger?"

"Yes, I did. I was an all-state point guard in high school, and I played for Union College for four years."

"No desire to go pro?"

"I didn't have the height, speed, or quickness to play at the pro level, even though I had the knowledge of the game. I realized I was more suited to coach than play."

"I felt I would have made it to the NFL or NBA if it weren't for my knee injury. I ran a four-three in the forty-yard dash, and I had a forty-four-inch vertical."

"With that kind of athleticism, you would have definitely written your own ticket. So, what part of California are you from?"

"I'm from Compton, and I joined the Marines to escape the gangs. I beat a guy half to death for beating on my sister shortly after high school—it turned out that he was part of the *Bloods*, and they were going to kill me if I didn't leave Compton."

"Have you been back home since then?"

"Yeah, plenty of times. After what I've seen in Iraq, I'm not afraid to die anymore, and besides, the guy I beat up was killed five years ago in a drive-by shooting."

"What did you see in Iraq?"

"The blood...the carnage...I saw that stuff on a regular basis. I was standing maybe a few yards or so from one of the guys in my unit. We cleared the street and secured the area, or so we thought. Moments afterward, he was shot in the head by one of the Iraqi militants with an M16 rifle. The whole top of his head was blown off, and I still have nightmares about that day."

"Is that why you drink whiskey and smoke marijuana so much?"

"Yeah, I get drunk and high every day to numb the pain and avoid having nightmares. I'm so jacked up mentally that I couldn't function at a regular nine-to-five gig without wanting to beat the brakes off anybody who disrespected me."

"I didn't come close to any type of combat in Desert Storm. My only battle was withstanding the 120-degree heat and dodging scorpions. Listen, I know somebody who can talk to you about your nightmares."

"Who...a shrink? I'm not crazy."

"No, I'm not saying you're crazy. You remind me so much of Brock...believe it or not, you two have a lot in common."

"Yeah, more than you know."

"What do you mean by that?"

"Nothing..."

"Then why are you doing this, man? It's obvious that you have some intelligence about yourself."

"I did have a decent life before this, but sometimes life has a funny way of beating you down. I didn't choose this...it's more like it chose me. Before I knew it, I was in too deep."

"Look, everyone needs help dealing with problems at some point in his life. I talked to my therapist years ago after the death of my wife, Brock's mother. She helped me deal with my grief."

"I get it. I just might have to take you up on that someday."

"Well, if I make it out of here alive, I'll give you my therapist's name and number. Hey, I think I'm ready for that bathroom break now."

"Sure, no problem."

The hit man driver unlocked Brent's handcuffs, and Brent went to the restroom to relieve his bladder. His plan was to get inside his head by pretending to be his ally and possibly turn him against the other hit man. He felt he needed him as an ally, just in case things got really bad for Brock and him.

"What's your name, if you don't mind me asking?" Brent asked.

"I do mind you asking," the hit man driver replied, "so let's just keep this all business from here on out, okay?"

"Understood."

Chapter 8

The traffic on Interstate Fifty-Seven was very heavy, and I knew we wouldn't reach Manteno before seven o'clock. Will was trailing me with his music blaring—he was about a hundred yards behind me, and I could still hear the bass of his sound system shake the entire frame of his BMW X5 truck. We were forty minutes in, and we hadn't reached 167th Street yet, when my stepfather's cell phone rang. It was Junior—I knew he wouldn't stop calling until he got an answer.

"What's up, BJ?" I asked.

"Where the hell are you, and why isn't Dad picking up?" Junior asked me.

"I'm stuck in traffic on the expressway. I'll be there soon."

"Alright. Hurry up, and I'll see you in a few."

I dodged a bullet because I hadn't figured out how I was going to tell Junior that Dad was missing—his visceral response to this was a guaranteed tirade, I thought. I have been known to be a hothead at times—but Junior's temper was ten times worse than mine.

The flow started to pick up once we passed 167th Street, but there was one prick in the left-hand lane moving very slowly and holding up traffic. I got on his bumper to make him speed up to no avail, so I finally went around to pass him in the right-hand lane.

It was a little past seven when I pulled up in my stepfather's driveway. Will was right behind me—his loud music surely disturbing the neighbors nearby.

"Turn that music down, man!" I shouted. "This isn't the damn ghetto!"

"I'm sorry, Brock," Will said. "I got a little carried away because Jay-Z's cut is my joint, man."

"Whatever, man. I need to figure out how to tell BJ that Dad got kidnapped."

"Just tell him the truth. You know he's going to blow up at first, but he'll calm down once you explain everything to him."

"You're probably right. Let's go inside."

As we walked toward the house, I couldn't help but marvel how majestic it looked—a two-story house with six bedrooms, hardwood floors, marble counter tops and twenty-foot-high ceilings. The grass was perfectly manicured, and the entire property resembled something out of a home and garden magazine. I turned my key in the lock, and we walked in. Junior was waiting for us in the living room.

"What's he doing with you, and where's Dad?" Junior asked.

"It's a long story, BJ, and you might want to fix yourself a stiff drink for this," Will answered.

"What happened?" Junior asked. "Is there something wrong?"

"Dad and I got jacked today," I answered solemnly. "Two guys pulled a gun on me and kidnapped Dad, and they want a million dollars by Friday at midnight or else he's good as dead. Some dirty cop contracted them for the job, so going to the police isn't an option."

"Jacked?" Junior asked. "Damn, I can't do anything with this low jack on my ankle. One million dollars...you have to give it to them, Brock."

Junior wasn't his usually contentious self and was surprisingly calm, considering the circumstances. Maybe he's grown since his time in prison, or maybe it hasn't truly registered yet that our dad was being held captive.

"I've got two hundred fifty grand right now," I said, "but I can't cash in my stocks until Monday. I have to find another way to get the rest of the money by tomorrow night."

"I've got a plan to get the other half," Will said. "I know a drug dealer who will loan you the money. This dude is making money hand over fist in these streets, dawg."

"I don't know about that, Will," I said. "I'm already waist deep in it with a dirty cop and two hit men, and now you want me to break bread with a drug dealer?"

"Do you have a better idea?" Will asked.

"Stop right there," Junior said. "This plan of yours sucks, Will. Hell, you might as well ask him, could he front us a *brick* on consignment."

"Why does my plan suck, BJ?" Will asked. "The money doesn't know where it comes from."

"Someone as simple-minded as you would say something like that," Junior said. "Quite frankly, I don't know why Brock still hangs out with you."

"Shut up, BJ," Will said.

"Both of you shut up," I said. "We're supposed to come up with a plan together, not fight."

"I'm cool, man," Will said.

"I'm not sorry about what I said because it's the truth," Junior said. "I don't care if he's mad."

"Whatever, BJ," Will said angrily.

"You do know there's a such thing as a moral clause in Brock's contract, don't you?" Junior asked. "He can't be associated with any known criminals or else the team can void his contract."

"I didn't know," Will said.

"It figures," Junior retorted.

"Look, you two, we're in a crisis situation right now," I said. "I could really use some help without all this damn bickering."

"I have some jewelry worth about 100K that I lifted off some rival drug dealers before I went to the pen," Junior said. "I have Rolex watches, platinum chains, and some rings in storage."

"You robbed some drug dealers?" I asked. "Man, you're crazy, BJ. I'll see if I can borrow some money from Malik, too."

"Sounds like you got everything covered, brother," Will said. "I'm gonna bounce."

"Wait, Will," I said. "I'm going to need someone to watch my back when I cash in this jewelry. I don't feel comfortable carrying that kind of money around."

"Consider it done," Will said. "When do you want to do it?"

"We can go in the morning," I answered. "I'll pick you up at nine."

"Alright, I'll clear my morning schedule and see you later," Will said, turning toward Junior and looking at him with contempt. "BJ."

"Wilbur," Junior said with an equal amount of disdain.

Will walked out and shut the door behind him. I looked at Junior as he shook his head with an intense look on his face.

"I can't stand him, man," Junior said. "Look, I know you don't like people telling you what to do but take some advice from your younger brother. Will has never had your best interests in mind, and I could see it...even as a kid. He's jealous of you for who you are and what you have."

"So, what are you really saying, BJ, that I should cut him loose?" I asked.

"That's exactly what I'm saying. I know people should be loyal to their friends through thick and thin, but Will is as shady as they come. I never told you this because I was afraid of getting in the middle of your friendship with him years ago."

"What are you talking about?"

"I was fifteen at the time, and it was about two weeks before your graduation. I was with my friend Anthony, and we were walking home from baseball practice when I saw Will and your ex-girlfriend Michelle hugging and kissing in the Walgreens parking lot on Eighty-Seventh and Stony Island. He didn't see me, and I never said anything about it. I realize now that I should have said something sooner."

"You don't have anything to be sorry about because it wasn't your fault. Everybody could see that he was only out for himself, but why couldn't I see it? I'm going to keep this under wraps for now because I need him to watch my back tomorrow. That explains why Michelle became distant and eventually broke up with me in the summer after high school graduation."

"I'm only trying to help you see the truth about him, and he's not worth beating yourself up about it."

"I know. I was just thinking about how I can't seem to keep a woman. I've had two meaningful relationships in my life that both ended in disaster."

"Don't beat yourself up about that, either. You made the mistake of picking two women who weren't really your type. You're a generous person, bro. Both of your ex-girlfriends were stuck-up and selfish, and they both took advantage of your kindness. Face it, man, you place too much stock in looks and not enough stock in substance."

Junior was right. Michelle was narcissistic and flighty, and she could be downright vicious at times. She was the captain of the cheerleading squad and the most popular girl in school, and she didn't hesitate to let everyone know it. Stephanie, on the other hand, was a pampered princess, who came from a rich and controlling family. She encroached my boundaries on a regular basis, and she expected me to cater to her every whim. I made a promise to myself that, the next time I fell for someone, it would be the real thing—not an illusion of the perfect relationship.

"I can't disagree with anything you just said, BJ," I said. "How in the hell did you get so wise?"

"A five-year jail term helped me see the light."

"Better late than never."

"Indeed."

Junior paused and then said, "Hey, what about Nikki and Jaz? Should we tell them about Dad?"

"No, that's not a good idea." I answered. "There's no sense in worrying them about this. Nikki and Jaz can't help us from opposite sides of the country. We're going to get him back tomorrow, and we can tell them afterwards."

"Alright, Brock."

I kicked off my shoes, tossed my jacket on the couch, and said, "I'm going to call it the night. See you in the morning."

"Hold up, bro..."

"What's up?"

"Give me a minute to find the key to my storage unit."

"Okay."

"So, where do you have to meet these clowns tomorrow?"

"On some baseball diamond in the warehouse district off 126th and Torrence."

I went to the fridge and grabbed a beer while Junior went to his room to find the key to his storage unit. I had turned my life over to God at the end of my second year in the league and was living a clean life up to now, but I gave in to the desire to backslide due to the stress of what happened earlier in the day. Junior came back to the living room and handed me the key a few minutes later.

"My storage unit is at Life Storage in Orland Park, and my unit number is 615."

"Cool."

"I also have 75K in cash there... I didn't want to reveal that in front of Will. It's bad enough that he knows about the jewelry because I don't trust him."

"Understood."

"Do me a favor, Brock."

"What is it?"

"Don't take Will with you tomorrow because you don't owe him nothing."

"Who else can I take with me, BJ? I can't take you with me because you're on house arrest."

"Take Malik with you."

"No way, man, I'm not going to put him in danger...what if something happens to both of us? What would the organization do if both of us get smoked?"

"This ain't about the damn organization. This is life and death bro, and you have to play the hand you're dealt in this game."

"I'll think about it."

"You do that. Goodnight."

"See you in the morning."

Chapter 9

I tossed and turned all night long—restless from Thursday morning events. I finally got out of bed at about seven, and I took a shower, brushed my teeth, and got dressed. Junior was still asleep, so I tried to be as quiet as possible.

I had a full morning on my plate that consisted of picking up Will, getting Junior's jewelry and cash out of his storage unit, and liquifying the jewelry at a pawnshop. I also have to get my money out of the bank at Chase after pawning Junior's jewelry. He had rented his storage unit with a fake alias right before the Feds seized his drugs, guns, and cash at the apartment he rented in the southwest suburbs. The jewelry and cash were the only remnants left from his life of crime.

I left the house at eight—I decided not to take Junior's advice and headed to the southeast side of Chicago to get Will. It was the middle of rush hour, so I got off the Interstate at 127th Street to avoid the backup. I went eastbound to Halsted and northbound on Halsted to Eighty-Seventh. Will lived two blocks from Jesse Owens Park on Eighty-Eighth and Luella Avenue. I pulled up in front of his house at eight fifty-five and got out the car to ring his doorbell. I stood on his porch for about thirty seconds before he answered the door.

"On time as usual," Will said, grabbing his morning paper and tossing it inside the house.

"I've got a lot of running around to do this morning, and time isn't on my side, Will," I said. "I've got less than twenty-four hours to come up with this money."

"Did you remember to call Malik?"

"I'm going to call him as soon as we head over to Junior's storage unit to get the jewelry."

"Okay."

"I need you to watch my back while I search for a pawn shop to cash in this jewelry, and then I'm going to drop you off at the barbershop. I know you have clients scheduled, and I don't want to tie up your day."

"It's cool, Brock. I cleared my schedule today, so if you need me for anything else, let me know."

"Alright."

Something in my gut didn't feel right, and my instincts have never failed me before. Will's extreme helpfulness had me bothered somewhat. It was totally out of character for him to offer anything, unless you asked him. He was the type of person who had the propensity to take, instead of give. I realized, at that moment, I didn't trust him anymore because of what Junior had told me last night.

I decided moments later that it was a good time to call Malik about borrowing the money. He picked up on the first ring.

"I see you're up already," I said.

"Yeah, Tanya and I are about to go to breakfast in about thirty minutes," he said. "What do you have going on today?"

I told him what happened, and there was dead silence for a moment.

"Did you say kidnapped?" he asked. "Why didn't you go to the police?"

"It's a long story," I answered. "Some dirty cop is responsible for this, so I can't involve the police. I'll fill you in with the rest of the details later. Also, I'm possibly going to have close to a half-million dollars by noon, and I need to borrow the other half from you today. I'll pay you back next week because I can't cash in any of my stocks until Monday."

"Sure, man, anything you need. I won some money on the boat last night, and I can get the rest from my bank. How much do you need exactly?"

"Six hundred thousand. Get it in hundreds, and I'll meet you at my house at one o'clock."

"Consider it done. I'll see you later."

I disconnected the call and gave my undivided attention to the road. I didn't have much to say to Will—finding it extremely arduous to weigh the pro and cons of my friendship with him and deciding whether to remain friends. We've been through a lot together, and it would have been very hard to throw eleven years away over a girl who broke up with me years ago.

"Why are you so quiet?" Will asked.

"I've got a lot on my mind, man," I replied. "I need to know something."

"What?"

"Why haven't you told me about Michelle, you damn hypocrite?"

"Michelle...what about her? I haven't seen her since high school."

"Don't play dumb with me. BJ saw you hugging and kissing her in the Walgreens parking lot right before high school graduation."

"I'm sorry, man. I just didn't know how to tell you..."

"I'm sick and tired of hearing you say sorry, Will. I can't believe, in seven years, you couldn't figure out a way to tell me the truth."

"I know it's no excuse. I should have told you, but the longer I waited, the more difficult it got. I was young and stupid, and I let Michelle's beauty cloud my judgement. I hope you can forgive me someday."

"I don't know, man. It makes me wonder if you're harboring more secrets. Maybe BJ is right about you...you only care about yourself and screw everybody else."

"That's not true, Brock. You're my man through thick and thin. I would never disrespect or betray you ever again."

"Alright, let's drop it. We were all very young, and everybody makes mistakes. Besides, I was eventually going to break up with her anyway because we were having problems our entire senior year."

"So, you're gonna let bygones be bygones?"

"Yeah, man, it's water under the bridge. I just needed to get it off my chest."

I'm not the type of person who gets off by seeing someone beg. Once I'm able to vent, I'm done with it. I didn't hold a grudge against him because I wasn't too mad about the circumstances anyway.

Junior's storage unit was located in Hyde Park, and it was always a hassle to find parking. Once we got there, I had to circle the block three times before a parking space opened up.

"Are you coming inside or staying in the car," I asked.

"Go ahead. I'll stay here and sightsee," Will answered.

"Alright. I'll be back in a minute."

I was able to park about a half block away from the place, and I briskly walked toward the front entrance. I passed this gorgeous young lady dressed in a tight-fitting, navy-blue blazer, a short skirt, and three-inch heels that accented her shapely calves. She was exiting the store as I was walking in, and we both turned around simultaneously to get a quick glance at each other. I smiled at her, but I was pressed for time and couldn't small talk. She smiled back, appearing to be in a hurry, also.

I walked over to one of the clerks, and I greeted her and asked, "Hi, can you help me?"

"Good morning, sir," the young lady replied and asked, "How can I help you?"

"I need to know where unit 615 is. It's been a while seen I've been here."

"Sure, follow me.

"Thank you."

She led me to a hallway and pointed toward the end of it before saying, "Unit 615 is the last one to your right."

"Thanks again."

"You're welcome."

Junior was smart enough to pay his bill yearly, instead of paying on a monthly basis. He was sentenced three years but only did eighteen months for good behavior, and Dad paid his bill for the following year, so it wouldn't lapse.

I then turned the key into the lock and opened the door. Junior had watches, chains, rings, and seven and a half bundles of one hundred dollar bills stored inside a medium plastic tote just like he said. There were other miscellaneous items inside the storage unit, like a tote full of clothing, a tote full of shoes, an iron and ironing board, furniture, and a toolbox. It was almost as if he knew he was going to get pinched, so he stored what he believed were items he'd need in the future.

I scooped the jewelry and cash out of the tote and placed them in an empty laundry bag that Junior conveniently had in storage. I then waved at the two clerks as I was leaving the store and walked briskly in the direction where I had parked, and I saw Will trying to get some young lady's phone number. He couldn't control his salacious impulses as I overheard him trying to convince the young lady to come to his house with some lewd comments.

"I see not a whole lot has changed, Will," I said.

"Excuse my manners, sweetheart," he said. "This is Brock."

"How are you," I said, shaking her hand.

"And this is Connie," he said.

"Nice to meet you, Brock," she said.

"Likewise," I said.

"We're pressed for time, Connie," he said. "I'll call you tonight when I get home, okay?"

"That's fine, Will," she said. "I'll talk to you later."

She turned to me, smiled and said, "Bye, Brock, it was a pleasure meeting you."

"Take care, Connie," I said.

Both of us watched her stroll west down Fifty-Third Street toward more restaurants and boutiques. She was very sexy, but she looked like a handful. Will always seemed to gravitate to trouble, and he craved racy women.

"I overheard your conversation with Malik, and you told him you had almost a half-million in cash," Will said. "BJ said he had a hundred grand in jewelry, and you said you had two hundred fifty grand yesterday. What else did BJ have in his storage unit?"

"You just cut to the chase, don't you?" I asked, evading his question.

"Come on, Brock, what gives?"

"If you must know, Junior had some cash in addition to the jewelry in storage."

"How much cash?"

"Calm down, man...why are you so thirsty?"

"Look, I am here for you, bro. I'm hoping for the best possible outcome in this situation, and I just want to make sure we have enough money to get this dirty cop off your back."

"He had seventy-five grand in there. I hope this jewelry is worth as much as he says it is."

"What pawnshop do you want to go to first?"

"I don't know yet. I do know I need to get top dollar for this jewelry, though."

"Why don't we go to the one on 79th and Jeffery?"

"Okay. Have you ever pawned anything there?"

"No, but I pass by there all the time, and there's always traffic at that location."

"Okay, let's do it."

Chapter 10

Brent was starting to get restless and wanted to be free of being handcuffed to the headboard. He knew in his mind that risking his children's lives, as well as his own life, by trying to escape wouldn't be an intelligent thing to do. However, Brent hadn't succeeded in convincing either assassin that the handcuffs were unnecessary.

The hit man driver left at a few minutes past eleven o'clock to walk Spike, the Rottweiler, and pick up a few items at the neighborhood grocery store. The other hit man was watching the eleven o'clock news, while Brent was trying to make small talk with him.

"Were you in the same unit as your partner-in-crime in Iraq?" Brent asked.

"No, I wasn't," the hit man passenger answered dryly.

"Where are you from?"

"Enough with the damn questions. I don't mix my personal life with business."

"Fine by me. If you don't feel like talking, it's okay."

"No, Brent, I don't feel like talking. Do me a favor and shut up while I try to watch the news."

"Fine, suit yourself. Before you get too comfortable, can you unlock the cuffs, so I can take a leak, please?"

"No, I'm watching the news right now. You can wait until it's over or pee in your pants... you choose."

"Hey, man, that is the last time you will disrespect me. Please unlock these handcuffs and let me use the bathroom."

"Go to hell, pops."

"Alright, my man," Brent said in calm, cool, and collected tone. "I'll wait."

"I thought you might see it my way," the hit man passenger said sarcastically.

"Well, you're the man with the gun," Brent added, "and that's the only thing stopping me from breaking your neck."

"You better watch your mouth, Brent," the hit man passenger said as he pulled out his gun.

"Kill me, and you won't get paid."

The other hit man walked in with the dog as his cohort pointed his nine-millimeter at Brent's head. The dog playfully began brushing his head against the hit man driver's leg.

"Yo, man, what the hell are you doing?" the hit man driver asked.

"I needed to use the bathroom, but your man wouldn't unlock the cuffs," Brent answered.

"I didn't ask you," the hit man driver said. "Yo, man, put the gun away."

The hit man passenger lowered his gun and said, "If he pops off at the mouth again, I'm gonna stop his clock."

"Calm down, fam," the hit man driver said. "We ain't gonna shoot nobody. Besides, we don't get paid if he's dead."

"Can one of you please unlock the cuffs, so I can take a leak?" Brent asked.

The hit man driver unlocked the handcuffs and said, "Go ahead. And the next time he needs to use the bathroom, fam, just let him. All this dumb stuff is totally unnecessary."

"Whatever, man," the hit man passenger said.

Brent scurried to the bathroom and barely got his pants unzipped before urinating in the toilet. The two hit men never referred to each other by name—carefully using pronouns and street jargon in reference to one another.

"Are these handcuffs really necessary?" Brent asked, as he dried his hands with a paper towel. "Where am I going to run?"

"We're very thorough, Brent," the hit man driver said. "We don't cut corners, and we don't make mistakes. I like you, but I'm still not taking any chances."

"I don't like you," the hit man passenger added as he handcuffed Brent's wrist to the headboard. "You try any funny business, and I'm gonna body you."

"Enough of that, fam," the hit man driver said.

"You and I will have our moment together," Brent said. "I promise."

"You better shut your smart mouth, old man," the hit man passenger said.

"I said, enough!" the hit man driver shouted. "Grab yourself a beer and chill, fam... it's too damn early for this."

Chapter 11

It was almost eleven fifteen when I parked half a block from the pawnshop on 79th and Jeffery Boulevard. I checked the perimeter for any strange people or suspicious activity once I stepped out of the car, and Will followed my lead after I transferred the cash from the laundry bag to my glove compartment. There were a couple of guys idly standing in front of the store, and one of them was begging for spare change. Another guy zoomed past us as we walked toward the pawnshop, and seconds later, a young woman yelled, "Somebody please stop him! He snatched my purse!"

Will took off after him and tackled him at the Walgreens across the street from the pawnshop. He then pulled out his gun and began pistol-whipping the thief. The young woman and I got there moments later.

"Chill out, Will!" I shouted. "You're gonna kill the dude!"

"This little punk picked the wrong one today, man!" he yelled back at me.

I pulled Will off him and said, "Put that gun away before somebody calls the police. I'm sure somebody videotaped you beating the crap out of this guy."

The young lady saw her purse on the ground next to the young man lying in a pool of his own blood leaking from his nose and mouth and said, "Thank you so much. My whole life is in this purse."

"You're welcome, Miss," Will said. "Glad I could help."

The young man slowly got off the pavement with his hand covering his nose and mouth, and I said, "You better get out of here before I call the police, my man."

"Gimme my purse, you lowlife bum!" the young woman shouted as she began pounding on the guy.

Will pulled her off him in an effort to calm her down. Bystanders began snickering and pointing at us, and I knew at this point it was time to go. I was uncomfortable with the laundry bag full of jewelry in my hand and gestured for Will and me to ditch the scene. Someone then called out my name as Will and I rushed to the car.

"Hey, Brock!" a man shouted. "Brock Lane...can I have your autograph?!"

We hopped inside the car, and I sped off. I pounded my fist on the steering wheel and asked, "What the hell just happened?"

"I just reacted to the situation, Brock," Will answered. "I didn't mean for any of that to happen."

"I don't blame you, Will. It's just that I don't have a plan B, and I don't have time to find another pawnshop."

"Why not? This is the hood...there's gotta be another pawnshop nearby."

"Because we have to meet Malik at one o'clock at my dad's house in Manteno."

"Oh yeah, that's right. What are we going to do about getting the rest of the money?"

"I don't know, but we'll have to think of something fast."

Chapter 12

Junior had just finished his daily workout and was about to take a shower before the phone rang. He thought it might have been Brock, so he answered on the first ring.

"Hello?"

"Hi, Brent, it's me. Do you want me to come by and hang out with you today?"

"Hey, Melissa. I was going to call you, but I have a family situation right now that needs my immediate attention."

"What's wrong, baby?"

"I can't talk about it. The less you know, the safer you'll be."

"I'm a big girl, Brent. I can handle it."

"It's not a good time to talk or hang out right now. I promise I'll call you later on tonight."

"Okay, Brent. I'll be expecting to hear from you, and if you don't call, I'm going to show up at your front door."

"That won't be necessary, baby. I love you, and I'll talk to you later."

"I love you too. Bye."

Junior met Melissa Manchester on a dating site a year ago while he was in prison. She is a junior at SIU in downstate Illinois, majoring in journalism. They eventually fell in love and chatted online every day until Junior got released on house arrest.

Junior took a shower and got dressed before the doorbell rang. He assumed it was Melissa because she had called from her cell phone and rang the doorbell afterward on several occasions. He opened the door, and it was Malik standing there with a large silver titanium briefcase in his right hand.

"What's up, Malik," Junior said, extending his hand toward him.

"BJ," Malik said, greeting Junior with a firm handshake. "I've heard so much about you that I feel like I know you already."

"Not all bad things, I hope."

"No, man, your big brother thinks the world of you. I know I'm a little early, but the urgency of the situation made me rush over here."

"Yeah, time is running out on us. Hey, I want to thank you personally, man. My dad means everything to me, and your loan is a tremendous help to us."

"You don't have to thank me...Brock is like a brother to me, and I'll do anything for him. I'm glad to be in a position to help."

"I appreciate it, Malik. Do you want something to drink? We got pop, beer, water..."

"Give me a beer. It's the off season, and I'm going fishing."

"That's funny," Junior said laughingly. "The Rockets gave you guys hell."

"Yeah, especially Flash Tucker. It should be against the law to be able to move that fast. I promise a different outcome next year if we meet up with them again."

"Your team can start by drafting a true point guard. Brock's really a two guard, and let's face it—Brock is a good defender, but the organization couldn't possibly expect him to guard somebody as quick as Flash Tucker the entire playoff series."

"You're right, BJ, but we don't pick until the second round this draft because we traded away our first-round picks for the next two years. Our only hope is free agency."

"Anyway, I know you got something going on this weekend. I'm tired of being cooped up in this crib, so I might as well get the blow-by-blow details of some party or something."

"As a matter of fact, Brock and I have plans to go to a private party on the north side tomorrow. Some of the Bulls are throwing it, and there's going to be some top-choice women there."

"Sounds like a real blast, Malik. I want to hear all about it on Sunday because we are going to get my dad back safe and sound tonight."

"That's right, BJ, safe and sound."

Chapter 13

"Will that complete your order, Mr. Suggs?" Naomi asked.

"Sure, hon," he said. "If you can bring me a newspaper to read, I'd really appreciate it."

"No problem, I'll bring you one back with your coffee."

Naomi left to place the elderly man's order of bacon, waffles, and a cup of coffee. He ordered the same thing every morning without fail, and she catered to him and made him feel at home, no matter what kind of day she was having. She was on a first-name basis with practically all her morning customers. Sally was a schoolteacher, who would come in bright and early when her shift started, June, the bus driver, would flirt with her every morning while he ordered his eggs and grits, and Rich was a blind man with a Labrador Retriever, who loved their hash browns and buttermilk pancakes. She loved her customers, and if she missed a day, every one of them would ask about her.

She walked over to June's table to give him his bill and asked, "Did you enjoy your breakfast today?"

"I'd enjoy my breakfast every day as long as you're serving it to me," he answered.

"That's so sweet, June. Make sure you come back and see us again, okay?"

"You know I will. Make my day and go out with me this weekend."

"I wish I could, but I'm busy this weekend. My girl is coming to town, and we're gonna hang Saturday and Sunday. I might take a rain check next week if I don't have too much homework."

"I'm gonna hold to that, girl. See you later."

"Bye, June."

Naomi knew just what to say to keep June interested, even though she had no interest in going out with him. She thought he was a nice guy, but in her mind, no one measured up to Brock. He ruined it for every other guy who had approached her since college.

She had her favorite customers, but she also had customers from hell. She would try her absolute best to remain professional, but sometimes, the drama got the best of her. After June left, there was a woman who frequented the diner complaining about her eggs being too runny and her toast being too brown. Naomi had just taken away her lukewarm coffee and replaced it with another cup ten minutes prior to her tirade, and she had just about all she could take from her.

"Where's my food?" the woman asked. "I have somewhere to be in the next few minutes."

"They're working on it, ma'am," Naomi answered. "It should be too much longer...sorry for any inconvenience."

"Well they need to move a little faster," the lady said. "Every time I come here, there's always a problem."

"Would you like a donut or bowl of fruit while you wait?" Naomi asked.

"No, dammit," the lady rudely answered. "I just want what I ordered five minutes ago."

Naomi sighed and said, "You don't have to be so rude, ma'am. All I've shown you was respect, but you continue to be nasty to me."

"I don't think I like your attitude, young lady," the lady said. "Let me see your manager."

"I'll gladly get him for you," Naomi said angrily, "and I don't like your attitude either. I'm not gonna just let you talk to me like that."

Naomi then stormed away to the kitchen area to get Steve. She was preparing to go on her break once she snatched off her apron.

"I'm going on my break, Steve," she said. "That *lady* wants to speak to you."

"Damn, her again," he said. "I don't understand why she continuously goes out of her way to be such a pain."

"I can't take it anymore, Steve. I've tried everything I could to be nice to her, but she crossed the line this time. I don't know what else to do."

"Don't worry about it, Naomi. I'll take care of it. Go take your break."

"Thank you, Steve."

Steve ended up comping the lady's meal, while Naomi took a walk to calm her nerves. She was a regular, but difficult, customer who demanded things to be a certain way, and Steve had to do a song and dance every other week to keep this lady happy. He wanted to tell her to go straight to hell, but he also knew that plan of action would ultimately cost him his job. Just another typical day at the diner, he thought.

Chapter 14

I was anxious to set up this meeting and get my stepfather back home—wondering what I was going to do to occupy my time until midnight. We saw Malik's rental car parked in the driveway once we arrived on the block. It wasn't quite one o'clock yet, and I appreciated the fact that he rushed over here as soon as he could. When we stepped in the house, Junior and Malik were drinking beer and watching television.

"What's up, fellas," I said. "Do you remember Will, Malik?"

"Yeah," Malik said. "What's up, Will?"

"Nothing much, Malik," Will answered. "I'm just taking things day by day. What's up, Junior?"

"Will," Junior said, nodding his head. He seemed to be still angry from last night's argument with him.

"How much were you able to get out of the bank?" I asked Malik.

"I brought six hundred thousand, like you asked me to bring," Malik replied.

"I'll have three hundred twenty-five thousand total and the jewelry," I said, "but I didn't withdraw the cash or pawn the jewelry yet."

"That will put us at nine hundred twenty-five thousand," Junior said. "I don't know where a pawnshop is around here."

"I can just go back to the bank for the 75K," Malik said.

"You've done enough already," I said. "I'll think of something."

"Come on, man," Malik said, "we're in the NBA. It's not a good look to be in a pawnshop."

"He's right, Brock," Will said. "Let him get the rest of the money, and you can pay him back next week."

"Are you sure it's no trouble, Malik?" I asked.

"Nah, Brock, of course not," Malik answered.

"The closest Chase is in Park Forest," Junior said.

"Okay, give me an hour, and I'll be back," Malik said. "Are you coming with me, Brock?"

"Yeah, let's bounce," I replied. "Come on, Will. We'll follow Malik to the bank."

"What if these dudes kill you and Dad once they get the money?" Junior asked hypothetically.

"Don't even speak that into existence," I replied.

"But if these guys are really contract killers, Brock," Junior said, "I'm pretty sure they got paid up front and not only to kidnap Dad."

"What other choice do we have?" I asked. "We have to take what they said at face value...we can't go to the police because it's a dirty cop employing them. Besides, we don't even know their names."

"I doubt if these guys are going to kill you or your dad, Brock," Will said.

"How can you be so sure?" Junior asked.

"Because Brock is a high-profile individual," Will answered. "If one of you or both of you get killed, that's heat they definitely don't want."

"He's probably right about that," Malik said. "Every law enforcement agency in Illinois would be after them."

"Come on, fellas, let's go," I said. "We don't have another second to waste."

"Keep me posted, Brock," Junior said.

"No doubt, bro," I said. "I'll text you when we have all the money, and I'll text you right before the meeting to get Dad back."

"Are you headed to the city after the bank?" Junior asked.

"Yeah, it doesn't make sense to come back here," I answered. "I gotta drop Will off once we get to Chicago."

"Not a chance, bro," Will interjected. "I got your back whether you like it or not."

"Me, too, Brock," Malik added.

"Neither one of you is coming with me," I said. "I can't risk you all getting killed tonight."

Will showed his nine-millimeter tucked in his jeans and said, "I can handle myself, Brock. You're gonna need some backup, just in case this thing goes bad."

"He's right, Brock," Junior said. "You're gonna need somebody watching your back..."

"What, you agree with me, BJ?" Will asked.

"This isn't the time for jokes, Will," Junior answered.

"Okay, Will, you can back me up," I said, "but you're gonna hang out with your girl, Malik. Does Dad still keep his gun in his top drawer?"

"Yeah, let me get it for you," Junior answered.

"Well, if I can't tag along, you better keep me posted too," Malik demanded.

"Deal," I said, shaking Malik's hand.

Junior came back to the living room area with Dad's gun and said, "Don't pull it unless it's absolutely necessary, Brock. We don't need you going to prison like me."

"I'm not new to the game, bro," I said. "Later."

"Later," Junior said.

"Nice meeting you, BJ," Malik said.

"Yeah, likewise," Junior said. "Keep my brother safe, Will."

"I got you, BJ," Will affirmed. "I won't let anything happen to Brock without it happening to me first."

Chapter 15

Naomi was wrapping things up at the diner when she got a text from Cecilia to pick her up from the airport. The original plan was to get to one of the happy hour spots before the end of the workday for food and drinks, and then it was shop 'til you drop at Macy's. Her cell phone rang moments later, and it was her second job at Chili's Grill and Bar calling her.

"Can you work tonight?" her boss asked.

"I kind of have plans tonight," Naomi replied.

"I'm swamped right now and can really use your help, Naomi," her boss said. "If you can do this favor for me, I'd greatly appreciate it."

Naomi paused and asked, "What time do you need me to come in?"

"As soon as possible," he replied. "You can leave as soon as the rush dies down...which should be well before closing, I hope."

"Okay, give me about a half hour," Naomi said.

"Great, see you in a few," he said.

Naomi disconnected the call and tried to call Cecilia to let her know she couldn't pick her up from the airport because, in addition to working at her second job, the shop had to order a part to finish repairing her brakes by Saturday morning fifteen minutes prior, but Cecilia didn't answer. Naomi then sent her a text instead:

Hey CeCe, I won't be able to pick you up from the airport because my car is still in the shop, and I have to work at Chili's for a few hours. I'll hook up with you tomorrow.

Naomi clocked out and left the diner after she requested an Uber to take her to Chili's.

"See y'all next week," Naomi said.

"Bye, Naomi," one of the wait staff crew said.

"See you Monday," Steve said. "Thanks again, Naomi."

"You're welcome, Steve," she said.

She exited the diner and waited for her driver to show up. Her app indicated the driver was three minutes away, traveling eastbound on Sibley Boulevard. A black 2017 Dodge Charger entered the parking lot moments later, and she checked the license plate number to make sure it was the right driver.

"Are you Naomi?" the driver asked.

"Yes, I am," she replied. "How are you, Nate?"

"I can't complain," he answered. "You look very familiar to me. Did you go to Thornridge High School?"

"As a matter of fact, I did. And you were on the basketball team, right?"

"Yes, I was. You have a good memory, and you're still beautiful as ever."

"Thank you, Nate."

Nate exited the lot and turned right on Sibley Boulevard and headed eastbound to Torrence Avenue. Naomi fastened her seatbelt and asked, "How do you like doing Uber?"

"It's good," Nate replied. "I do it in my spare time to earn some extra money. I'm a manager at a warehouse in Bolingbrook, Illinois full-time in the shipping/receiving department."

"Hey, whatever pays the bills, right?"

"Absolutely. So, what do you do?"

"I'm a waitress at that diner you picked me up at, and I'm a waitress at Chili's in between going to school."

"Sounds like your plate is full."

"It is."

Nate paused briefly and asked, "What school do you attend?"

"I go to Roosevelt," Naomi replied, "and I'm six hours away from graduation after this semester."

"What's your major?"

"Accounting."

"That's great."

"So, how come you aren't playing basketball anymore?" she asked, changing the subject. "I followed your college career at DePaul, and I thought you were good enough to play basketball at the next level."

"Well, to make a long story short, I did play overseas for a couple of years before I traded in my Nikes for a regular life," he answered. "I was tired of being away from home, and once my son was born, I decided I wanted to move back to the States and be a full-time dad."

"Are you married?" she asked, noticing the band on his left ring finger.

"Yes, for two years now," he replied. "A blissful two years to a wonderful woman, I might add."

"Congratulations."

"Thank you."

Congestion was heavy on Torrence Avenue between 159th Street and Bernice Drive, and it usually was every day in the afternoon hours. It was bumper-to-bumper traffic at the River Oaks Mall, and traffic was stop and go.

"So, what about you?" he asked. "Do you have a significant other?"

"No, I'm afraid not," she replied.

"Really? I find that very hard to believe."

"Well, believe it. I just haven't met the right guy yet."

"I'm sure you will one day."

"I hope so."

Traffic finally opened up, and Nate entered the Chili's parking lot a few minutes later. He parked in front on the entrance and put his hazard lights on.

"It's was nice seeing you again, Naomi," he said. "Good luck with school and take care of yourself."

"Nice seeing you again as well, Nate," she said. "Take care."

"Bye."

She exited the car and entered the restaurant before she rated Nate's service. She gave him five stars and tipped him two dollars in addition to the six dollars and twelve cents fare she was charged. She was also slightly disappointed that Nate wasn't available because she found him to be very attractive. When will it be my turn to meet Mr. Wonderful, she thought.

Chapter 16

I trailed Malik to the Chase Bank branch in Park Forest, Illinois to withdraw the money to free Dad. I thought of a game plan for us to withdraw the remaining portion of the money together in order to avoid any type of suspicion. My plan was to tell the personal banker that our large withdrawals were for a property we jointly purchased, and I had to find out exactly what Malik told the bank this afternoon because we were going back to the same branch.

Malik entered the lot and parked his car in front of the bank. Another space wasn't available in the front of the bank, so I parked in the rear of the bank. Will and I then walked toward Malik standing next to his car.

"What's the game plan?" Malik asked.

I looked at my watch and saw it was a little after three o'clock, and I replied, "We can use the same personal banker you used before to get the rest of the money. What did you say the money was for?"

"I told the young lady I needed the money to purchase a rental property," Malik answered. "I figured we could say something like we need more money to close the deal."

"Perfect," I said. "I was just thinking the same thing...that we're buying a building jointly as real estate investors."

"That's a great idea," Will said. "We definitely don't want to draw any unwanted attention to ourselves."

"Come on, fellas, it's game time," I said. "You quarterback this thing, Malik."

"Okay, let's do it," Malik said.

We entered the bank, and the same personal banker who helped Malik the first time greeted the three of us in the front of the lobby. I tried to remain calm and let Malik do most of the talking because the last thing I wanted was the Press to find out about the two of us withdrawing a million dollars in cash from a banker who perceived our motives as suspect.

"Welcome back, Malik," the young, blond banker said, extending her hand to me first. "I'm Melody."

"Brock," I said, shaking her hand.

"I know," she said, smiling from ear to ear. "I'm a huge fan."

"Thank you," I said, "and this is Will."

"Nice to meet you, Will," Melody said.

"Nice to meet you too, Melody," Will said.

"What brings you back, Malik?" Melody asked.

"My business partner wants to go in with me and buy a bigger unit," Malik answered.

"That's great," Melody said. "Teammates and business partners—it doesn't get any better than that."

"Yes, and this will be the start of something great, I hope," Malik said.

"I'm going to wait in the lobby," Will said as he walked over to a row of seats and sat down.

"Let's get down to business, boys," Melody said. "As you probably know, we have to report cash withdrawals totaling ten thousand dollars or more to the IRS."

"Okay," I said.

"I know the drill," Malik added.

"Splendid," Melody said. "Can I have your driver's license, Brock?"

"Sure," I answered, reaching inside my wallet and handing my driver's license to her.

Melody went to print a copy of my license. She returned moments later and handed it back.

"How much do each of you want to withdraw?" Melody asked.

"Two hundred and fifty thousand dollars," I answered.

"And I need an additional eighty thousand dollars," Malik answered.

"Are you sure you don't want cashier's checks instead, gentlemen?" she asked.

"I'd prefer it that way, but our seller wants cash for some strange reason," Malik answered. "I think he wants to spread his deposits out over five banks and doesn't want to pay wiring fees."

"Very well," Melody said. "Give me your account numbers, so I can prepare your withdraw slips."

Malik gave Will the keys to his car, so he could get his titanium briefcase. Melody went to the vault to get our cash and returned with a black duffel bag just after Will came back with the briefcase. She then counted the thirty-three bundles in front of us, and Malik placed those bundles in the briefcase with the rest of the money.

"Good luck with the purchase of your first property together, guys," Melody said.

"And thank you for your time and patience," Malik said.

"Thank you," I said.

"It was no trouble at all, gentlemen," she said.

The three of us exited the bank and motioned toward Malik's car when I said, "That was quick thinking, Malik. I didn't know what to say when she asked about getting a cashier's check."

"Yeah, man, way to be quick on your feet, Malik," Will added.

"Brian Dawson of the Bulls had a similar experience when he owed a gambling debt," Malik said. "He didn't want to say what the money was really for, so he lied and said he wanted to withdraw it in order to buy a property."

"Because he didn't want the story to leak to the Press, right?" I asked.

"Exactly," Malik replied.

We continued to stand idly by Malik's car for a moment, and then Will asked, "So, what now, Brock?"

"I need a drink, man," I answered. "Let's go to the Chili's in Cal City."

"Cool," Will said. "They have that two for twenty-two deal going on."

"And that's all I can afford at this point," I added. "After I pay you back next week, Malik, I won't have two nickels to rub together until the start of the season."

"You can pay me back after training camp," Malik said.

"Are you sure?" I asked.

"Yeah, I'm good," Malik answered.

"Thanks, man, you have been a godsend to me," I said.

"No problem, Brock," Malik said. "You'd do the same for me."

"No doubt," I said, giving him some dap.

"You gonna roll with us?" Will asked.

"I wish I could, but I promised Tanya dinner tonight," Malik answered.

"Do your thing, bro," I said. "I'll call you when we get Dad back."

"Okay," Malik said. "Later, fellas."

Malik gave us both dap and drove off. We then hopped in my dad's car and headed toward I-57. My intention was to get as wasted as I possibly could, so I didn't become consumed with my date with destiny.

Chapter 17

"Do you want some pizza, pops?" the hit man driver asked.

"Yeah, I'll have a slice," Brent answered. "Thank you."

"No problem," the hit man driver said. "Yo, fam, you want some pizza?"

"Nah, man, I'm good," the hit man passenger answered. "You know I don't eat pork."

"Damn, my bad, fam," the hit man driver said. "I had a taste for some pizza and forgot. I can go back out and get you something else."

"Don't worry about it, fam," the hit man passenger said. "I'll grab something a little later... after we make this exchange. I'm gonna call Brock and check on his progress."

The hit man passenger grabbed his phone and asked, "What's Brock's number?"

Brent gave him Brock's number and added, "I'm sure he has the money."

"He better have it," the hit man passenger said before dialing the number.

"Who's this?" I asked.

"You got my money?" the hit man passenger asked.

"Yeah, I got your money," I answered. "Lemme speak to my dad."

"You ain't calling no shots here, bruh," he affirmed. "We're gonna up the time since you have the money."

"Why don't we change the place, too?" I requested. "No sense in meeting in a secluded place in broad daylight."

"No, we meet at the original spot," he demanded.

"I need some assurance that my dad is okay," I said.

"Let your son know you're alright, pops," he said.

"Hey, Son!" Brent shouted. "I'm okay!"

"You hear that, Brock?" he asked.

"Yeah, I heard him," I answered. "How do I know you're gonna let us go once I give you the money?"

"That's the million-dollar question, bruh," he answered. "Meet us at the spot in one hour and not a second later."

He disconnected the call, and I continued to drive in silence. Will looked at me and said, "What's going on, Brock?"

"They want me to make the drop in an hour," I answered. "Alone."

"Alone?"

"Yeah, alone. I'm gonna have to drop you off somewhere... can't risk them shooting us because we broke the rules."

"They're gonna pop you for sure without me watching your back, fam."

"That's a chance I'm gonna have to take. Where do you want me to drop you off?"

"You can drop me off at the next exit in Cal City at the McDonald's. I'll catch an Uber from there."

"Cool."

I exited the expressway at the Sibley Boulevard East and pulled up in the McDonald's parking lot. I stopped in front of the restaurant and said, "I'll call you once it's over, Will. Thanks for your help."

"You don't have to thank me," he said, giving me a firm handshake. "Talk to you later."

"Later, Will."

I exited the lot and made a left turn in the direction of Torrence Avenue once the traffic dissipated, and I rode in silence the entire way. The baseball diamond was empty, and nobody was outside at the industrial plant across the street. I then parked the car in one of the diagonal slots, and I took all but 5K of Junior's cash from the glove compartment and placed it Malik's briefcase with the rest of the money. After that, I bowed my head and said a prayer:

Thank you, Father God, for the many blessings you have given me and please forgive me for any sins I've committed since I've last spoken to you. I sent Will away because I trust you completely and know you will protect me. I praise you and thank you in the midst of my chaos in Jesus' name. Amen.

I sat of the hood of my dad's car and waited for the kidnappers to show up. Five minutes passed. Ten minutes...still no sign of them. Finally, after twenty-two minutes and about fifteen seconds, the decrepit, rust-colored Caprice slowly crept up to the spot where I'd parked and stopped right in front of me. I could barely see through the tinted windows that my stepfather was unharmed in the back seat.

The three of them got out of the car and stood a few feet away from the spot where I'd parked. My stepfather stood behind the two of them.

"You're on time," the hit man passenger said. "You see this, fam? That's what I call good business."

"Where's the money, Brock?" the hit man driver asked.

"It's in the car," I answered.

"Hand it over," the hit man passenger said. "Let's make this quick and painless."

"I'll hand it over when you release my dad," I said.

"Fair enough," the hit man driver said. "Open the briefcase and place it in front of your car. I'll let your dad go once we see the money."

I did what he instructed me to do, and the hit man passenger nodded at my stepfather once I placed the opened briefcase on the ground. My stepfather quickly walked toward me and turned around to face his captors.

"Now that was easy," the hit man passenger said as he walked toward the briefcase full of money and picked it up. "Is it all there?"

"It's all there," I answered. "Count it if you don't believe me."

"No need, Brock," the hit man passenger said. "I like your style."

"I held up my end of the bargain," I said. "Are we free to go?"

"Yeah, you're free to go," the hit man driver answered. "But if I get wind of you going to the cops, I'll kill your whole family, starting with you, pops."

"1217 Katlyn Drive, right?" the hit man passenger asked rhetorically.

"I hear you," I said, "but this is a one-time deal. You won't catch me slippin' again."

"Is that a threat, bruh?" the hit man passenger asked as he pulled out his gun.

"No, it's a promise," I answered, pulling out my stepfather's gun from my pants. "Don't let the smooth taste fool you."

"Brock's got balls," the hit man driver said. "Put your gun away, fam."

"Nah, I'm gonna teach him a lesson," the hit man passenger said.

"No, we're gonna call it even, fam," the hit man driver said. "Y'all get outta here before I change my mind."

I tucked the gun back in my pants once the hit man passenger lowered his gun, and my stepfather and I got in the car. I didn't dare look the gift horse in the mouth and burned rubber westward down 126th Street.

Chapter 18

I turned left on Torrence Avenue, without waiting for the light to turn green, and continued south. My stepfather finally broke his silence and said, "Well done, Son. How did you come up with that kind of money so fast?"

"I had help from Malik," I answered. "I don't have that kind of cash on hand."

"I know... your contract extension doesn't kick in until next season."

"Right."

I continued southward on Torrence Avenue once I crossed 130th Street, and my stepfather asked, "You're not taking the expressway?"

"Nah, I want to go to Chili's to clear my head. You can drop me off and head home."

"You don't want company?"

"I'm good. The question is, are you okay?"

"I'm fine, Brock. I was handcuffed to the bed the whole time, though. My wrist is a little sore; that's all."

"Those dudes are lucky I know the Lord."

My stepfather paused for a moment and said, "I've had a couple of days to think about this, and I've come to the conclusion that we've been duped."

"Duped?" I asked. "How?"

"There was no dirty cop involved, and those guys weren't hit men."

"How can you be so sure, Dad? I couldn't just gamble with your life."

"And I'm eternally grateful you didn't gamble with my life, but I can't help but wonder how they knew so much about us."

"So, you're saying it wasn't a dirty cop extorting us?"

"No, I don't think so, Brock. They were privy to information that only you and I knew. I think someone in your circle helped them."

"Someone in my circle? I don't have that many friends..."

"Not your immediate circle...maybe it was somebody from your past. As you very well know, you hung with some shady people once upon a time."

"You're right, but who could it be?"

"I don't know, but your contract extension is public knowledge, and anyone can gain access to your information these days. You might want to consider hiring a bodyguard."

"That's not my style, Dad. I want to be free to do whatever I want when I want."

"You might not have a choice... what would stop them from striking again? You have to be proactive on this."

"Nothing would stop them. Maybe we should contact the police."

"I'm one step ahead of you. I have a friend in the police department that served in the Gulf War with me. I'm going to give him their license plate number."

"*MR GRIM*... so much for anonymity."

"Well, they weren't dumb criminals because they never referred to each other by name. However, they weren't professionals either. Your money is a come-up for them... nothing more, nothing less."

"What you're saying makes perfect sense. So, what's your cop friend's name?"

"His name is Blaine Stanton, and he's the best at what he does."

"Where did they take you?" I asked as I turned into the Chili's parking lot.

"I don't know because they blindfolded and handcuffed me," he answered. "They didn't take them off until we entered their house, and they blindfolded and cuffed me on the way here."

I parked the car and reached in my pants for the gun. I made sure no one was watching before I handed it to my stepfather.

"Here, Dad," I said. "I don't have a license to own a firearm in Illinois, and I would never carry a gun under ordinary circumstances."

"Thankfully, you didn't let the gun laws stop you this time," he said.

My stepfather paused for a moment and said, "Did you recognize the driver?"

"No," I answered. "Why do you ask?"

"Because I told him he had a lot in common with you when he said he played football and basketball in high school, and after I made that statement, he said 'more than you know.' I asked him what he meant by that, and he replied 'nothing.' That seemed rather strange to me."

"Now that I think about it, he kind of looks like this guy who lit up my high school team for forty points in a pre-conference tournament game senior year."

"What high school did he played for?"

"It was Compton High."

"Damn, he does know you because he said he was from Compton."

"Well, that explains part of the problem..."

"I promise you that we'll get to the bottom of this real soon."

"I'm certain we will. Hey, I'll take an Uber home when I'm done."

"Okay, Son, be careful."

"I will. See you later."

I got out of the car and went inside the restaurant. There were several empty seats at the bar, so I took one. A beautiful barmaid served me a shot of whiskey and beer, and that barmaid turned out to be Naomi Hill. She was a little angry at me because I didn't recognize her at first, and I was trying to think of a way to get back in her good graces before she brought back my second round of drinks.

"Thank you, Naomi," I said when she placed my drinks in front of me.

"So, you *do* remember me, huh?" she asked sarcastically.

"I'm very sorry, Naomi, but it's been a rough couple of days for me. I haven't slept since Wednesday."

"I'm sorry to hear that."

Naomi paused for a second and said, "I forgive you, Brock, but you're gonna have to make it up to me."

"Okay, maybe we could go out sometime soon," I said. "I'll be in town for a month."

"I'd like that. Don't go away...I have to serve some more customers."

"I'll be here."

Naomi tended to her other patrons, while I sipped on my drinks. Her smile made me feel better, so I ordered some bone-in chicken wings and fries.

"Are you sure that's all you want?" Naomi asked with a smile that seemed to light up the entire restaurant.

"I'll take your phone number as well," I answered.

"I thought you'd never ask," Naomi said as she grabbed my phone and programmed her number in it. "Make sure you see me before you leave."

"I most certainly will," I said.

Her smile still gave me butterflies in the pit of my stomach. I remember that smile vividly the first time we met. It was freshman orientation at Union College, and we were in the same meet-and-greet session headed by a couple of upperclassmen. We sat next to each other, and the smell of her perfume sent me into orbit.

We engaged in some small talk after orientation was over, and that's when I learned she had a boyfriend, who also attended the college and was a year ahead of us. Needless to say, I was heartbroken. I met Autumn not long afterwards, and I began dating her instead.

I sent Malik, Will, and Junior a group text and told them my stepfather was safe and sound, and I let them know he was on his way home. Naomi brought out my food about fifteen minutes later, and I'd finished my drinks.

"Do you want another round?" Naomi asked.

"No, thanks," I answered. "You can bring me a Coke instead."

"Okay, coming right up, sweetie."

I felt a warm sensation when she called me *sweetie*. Junior then responded to the group text first:

Great. Good work bro.

A preteen boy recognized me and asked for an autograph. I obliged him and gave his mom an autograph also. The crowd was beginning to pick up some more, and people were starting to gather around the bar where I was sitting. I took that as my cue to ditch the scene, and I didn't even get a chance to finish my food.

"Can you bring me the bill, Naomi?" I asked.

"Sure, Brock," she whispered in my ear. "I see what's going on, and I totally understand. Make sure you call me, alright?"

"Okay, I will."

Naomi leaned over and kissed me on the cheek, and the softness and fullness of her lips gave me goose bumps. I felt the vibration of my phone in my pocket, and Malik responded to the text next:

Glad to hear that Brock! Call me later when you get a chance.

Naomi brought over a hand-held device with a picture screen on it to make payment. I swiped my card and left her a very generous tip.

"I'll call you later on tonight," I said. "Bye."

"Bye, hon," she said. "I'll be looking forward to it."

I requested my Uber and waited outside. The app indicted that my driver was five minutes away, and I still hadn't gotten a response from Will.

Epilogue

"Let's tally up this money," Russell said. "This is the beginning of the life we've always talked about."

"Not yet," Terrence instructed. "We'll wait until Will gets here. Technically, this is his score."

"But we did all the work, so I say it's time to count this money."

"Slow your role, bruh. We would even have this money if it wasn't for him, so sit down and wait."

"Okay, boss, whatever you say. He's your boy, not mine."

"Yeah, he's my boy... he saved me from a guaranteed beating from some Bloods at a house party in Compton after my team beat his team in high school..."

"How many times are you gonna tell that story, fam? Look, he double-crossed his boy Brock, and it's only a matter of time before he crosses you."

"Come on, man, it ain't like that..."

"Then what is it like, huh? You can't trust him, Terrence, and I damn sure don't trust him."

"Man, he doesn't even like Brock, Russ..."

"Really? Then why does he still hang out with him?"

"Because he's rich, bruh. And that's how he got that barbershop up and running."

"Well, now we're rich too."

"Three hundred thousand is comfortable, not rich. We're gonna have to figure out what our next score is."

"We will cross that bridge when we come to it. You want a beer?"

"Yeah, grab me one."

There was a knock at the door before Russell could grab the two beers. Terrence answered the door, and Russell grabbed another beer as Will walked in the door.

"Sorry I'm late, fellas," Will said.

"Here," Russell said as he handed Will the beer.

"Thanks," Will said. "So, y'all ready to count this money?"

"Yeah, let's do it," Russell said as he handed Terrence a beer.

"Yo, I thought you were gonna be there?" Terrence asked.

"He didn't want me there," Will answered. "I thought y'all were gonna smoke Brock and his old man?"

"We needed you there to shoot Brock because he was gonna be the one with the burner, Will," Terrence answered.

"Yeah, we had to let them go because Brock pulled it out," Russell added. "And that also means one of us would've potentially gotten shot before we wasted him, and I'm not trying to die yet."

"Now, what if he traces the robbery back to me?" Will asked.

"You should've thought about that before you backed out," Russell said. "We should take it outta your cut."

"That's not gonna happen," Will affirmed.

"Relax, fellas," Terrence said. "We'll figure something out."

"We got enough money, so we should all disappear," Russell said. "I might even go back home to LA."

"That wouldn't be a good idea, Russ," Terrence said. "You're still wanted for murder, remember?"

"I was just kidding, fam," Russell answered.

"I can't go anywhere because they would definitely put two and two together if I disappear," Will said.

"That's your bag, bruh," Russell said. "There's nothing keeping us here once we split this money. If you go down, you keep our names outta your mouth, understand?"

"I ain't no snitch, Russ," Will said.

"Nobody's going anywhere," Terrence said. "We started this together, and we're gonna finish it together. We can also start planning our next score because this money isn't gonna last forever."

"We can start by figuring out a way to get our hands on his sidekick Malik's money," Will stated. "He's the one who funded most of this project."

"Yeah?" Terrence asked. "I thought Brock just signed that $150 million deal."

"Effective next season," Will answered. "Brock's damn near bankrupted after he cleaned out his bank account today."

"Man, that's messed up," Russell said. "We should've hit Malik in the first place."

"Okay then, it's settled," Terrence said. "Malik is our next target. Let's get to work on planning this thing."

73723591R00043

Made in the USA
Columbia, SC
06 September 2019